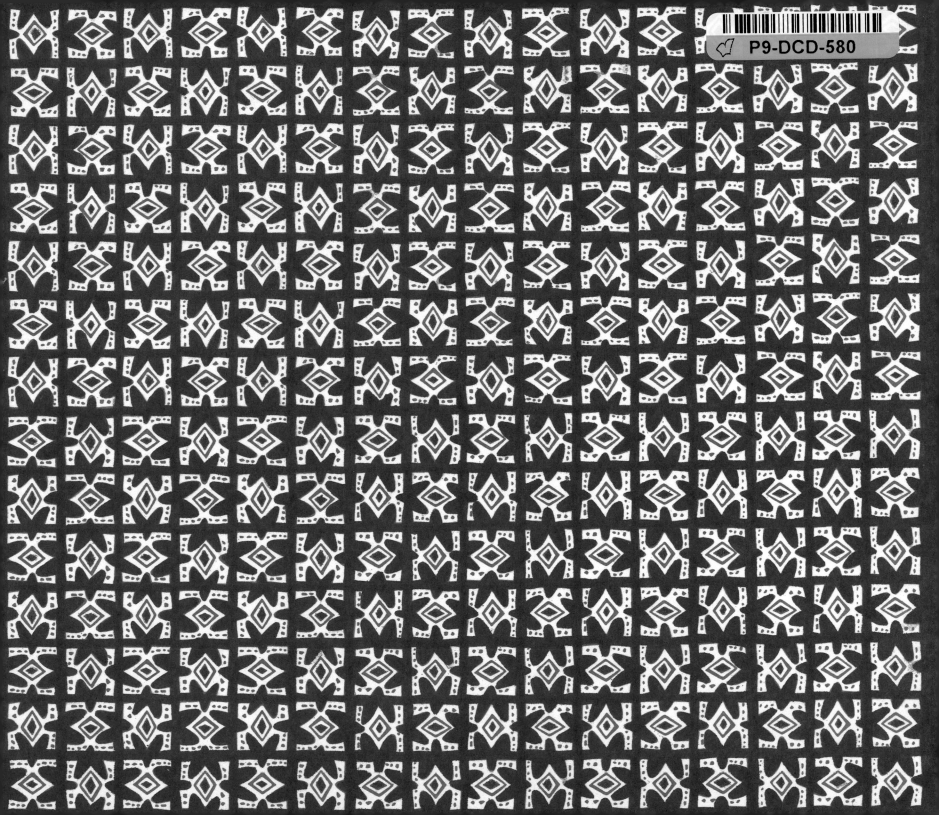

The King
and
The Tortoise

By Tololwa M. Mollel

Illustrations by Kathy Blankley

Clarion Books
New York

Clarion Books
a Houghton Mifflin Company imprint
215 Park Avenue South, New York, NY 10003
Text copyright © 1993 by Tololwa M. Mollel
Illustrations copyright © 1993 by Kathy Blankley

Printed and bound in Hong Kong

LIBRARY OF CONGRESS CATALOGING-IN-PUBLICATION DATA

Mollel, Tololwa M. (Tololwa Marti)
   The king and the tortoise/by Tololwa M. Mollel; illustrated by Kathy
Blankley.
      p.   cm.
   Summary: The king challenges the animals in his kingdom to prove their
wisdom by making him a robe of smoke, but only the tortoise is able to
satisfy him.
      ISBN 0-395-64480-1
      [1. Folklore — Cameroon.] I. Blankley, Kathy, ill. II. Title.
   PZ8. 1.M73Ki 1993
   398.21—dc20
   [E]
                                                           92-12485
                                                              CIP
                                                              AC

10   9   8   7   6   5   4   3   2   1

To Leona and Max Pinsky
—T. M.

To Tolo and to my Dad,
who would have been so pleased and proud
— K. B.

There was once a king who considered himself the cleverest person in the world. To prove it, he issued a challenge to all the creatures who lived in his kingdom:

"No one in my kingdom is cleverer than I am!" he said. "But if you think you are, you must prove it. Your task is to make me a robe of smoke. Anyone who can accomplish this will be declared the cleverest creature in the world."

News of the king's extraordinary challenge spread throughout the kingdom. His subjects came from near and far to watch the spectacle.

The king commanded that a huge fire be lit in the town square. Drumming and celebration filled the smoky air as the king and his councillors marched to their place of honor.

The first to accept the challenge was the hare. She jumped into the circle of spectators to wild applause. She did a little dance and a somersault to show off her nimbleness.

"I am swift of foot and of mind," bragged the hare. "The whole world sings about my tricky deeds! I, O noble king, will prove I am the cleverest in the world. I will make you a robe of smoke."

With these words she sped back and forth frantically, trying to clutch the smoke with her little paws. But, choking from the fire and gasping from the heat, she soon stumbled away exhausted. The crowd booed, and the king smiled a broad smile.

The next to accept the king's challenge was the fox.
The spectators shouted their approval.

"I was born sly and cunning," barked the fox. "What more
does one need for the task? I will make the king a robe of
smoke!"

Round and round the fire he spun, whipping the smoke into
shape with his tail. But, like the hare, he was overcome by the
smoke and he retreated to the great satisfaction of the king
and his councillors.

Now the leopard sprang into the square. The crowd roared.

"I am powerful and fierce! The lambs huddle in fear as I prowl the night. I will prove I am the cleverest in the world. I will make you, my king, a robe of smoke."

Leaping this way and that, the leopard growled and clawed at the smoke — but all in vain. He slunk away in defeat.

Then the earth shook. Into the square stomped the elephant, holding a pot high in his trunk. Whistles and cheers greeted him as he bellowed:

"My tread is heavy through the forest. Trees tremble at my approach. To be the cleverest creature in the world, all one needs is strength. I will make the king a robe of smoke."

With all his might, the elephant blew the smoke into his pot and covered it. Then the elephant bowed low before the king. With a flourish of his trunk he whisked the lid from the pot. But instead of the miracle robe, out came a huge billow of smoke.

The king and his councillors roared with laughter. The hare and the fox, the leopard and the elephant had all failed. Surely no one in the kingdom was cleverer than the king.

Now, nobody had seen the tortoise crawl slowly into the square. When the people finally noticed him, some in the crowd applauded. Others yelled at him to stop making a fool of himself. How could the slow tortoise succeed when others, more swift and sly, more powerful and strong, had failed?

The tortoise bowed his head before the king.

"I am neither swift nor sly, powerful nor strong, O noble king. But I can make you a robe of smoke."

Everyone laughed.

"Making a robe of smoke, O illustrious king," continued the tortoise, "requires not only a great deal of magical skill but much patience as well. So to fulfill the task may I, O most worthy king, request that you grant me seven days?"

"Your wish is granted, O greatest of magicians," replied the king indulgently. "You may have as much time as you wish."

"**J**ust one more thing, most noble king," said the tortoise. "You must promise that whatever I need for the task, you will provide."

"Whatever you ask," replied the king with a wink at the crowd, "I will provide."

"Upon your word?"

"Upon my word!" declared the king.

A week passed and the people gathered once again. They were sure the tortoise would be shamed when he appeared before the king. Slowly the tortoise hobbled into the square — empty-handed.

The crowd scoffed and hooted.

"It seems that making a robe of smoke has proven too difficult a task for you," observed the king. His enormous body shook with laughter. His councillors laughed with him.

The king felt very clever indeed to have devised such an impossible task.

But the tortoise did not leave the square. Instead, he lifted his head high.

"You need not worry, your majesty. You will soon have your robe," he said.

The king's laughter died in his throat. "I will?" he asked.

"Yes, most worthy king," replied the tortoise. "The robe is almost completed, but I ran out of thread. If your majesty would be kind enough to provide me with more thread, you will have your miracle robe in no time."

Once again, the king burst into merry laughter. He laughed so hard that he had to be supported by his councillors. The request for more thread was such a clever one that he decided to humor the tortoise.

"If that is all you need," the king replied cheerfully, "you can have all the thread in the world."

The king ordered that baskets of thread be put before the tortoise.

"**N**o, no, no!" cried the tortoise. "This will never do. It takes more than ordinary thread to finish a robe of smoke. To make a robe of smoke I need a thread of fire."

The councillors were dumbstruck. There was a murmur from the curious crowd.

For a long moment the king stared speechlessly at the tortoise. He was keenly aware of the watching eyes upon him.

Twice he opened his mouth. Twice no words came out.

Then slowly the king smiled his broad smile. In his full majesty he addressed the tortoise.

"I could easily provide what you need and more," said the king. "But alas, what is the use? I no longer need the silly robe. You have proven to me that you are clever enough to make one, and that is all I really wanted to know."

The king sighed a sigh of deep pleasure.

"Oh, how happy I am! In my kingdom live the two cleverest creatures in the world — you and I!"

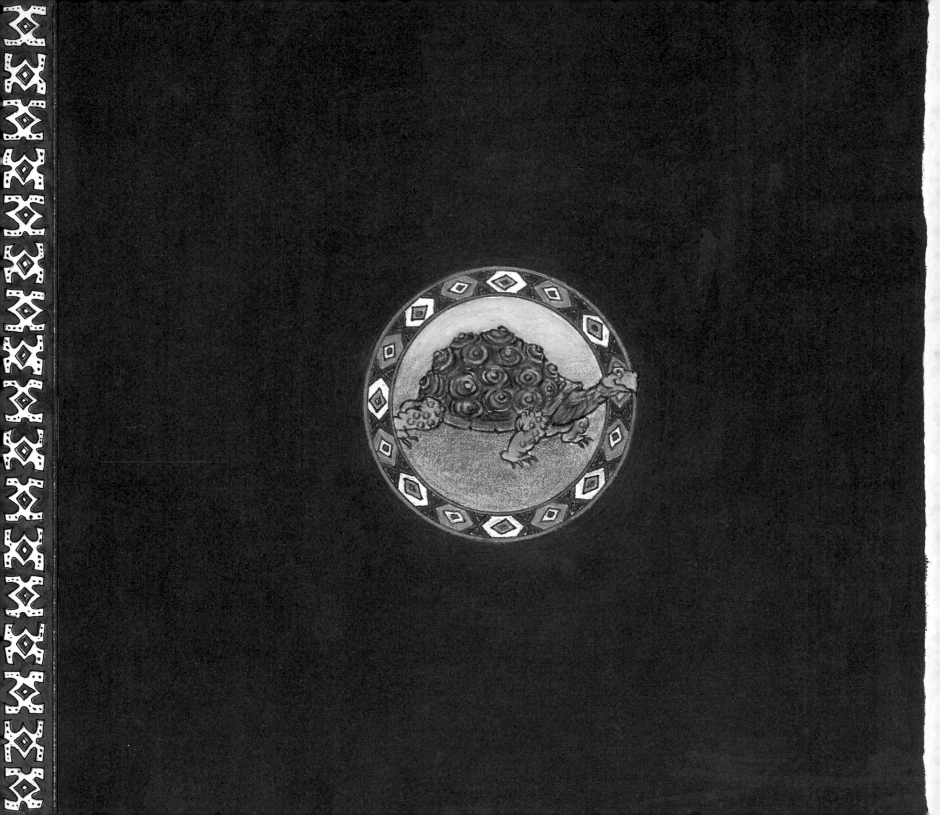

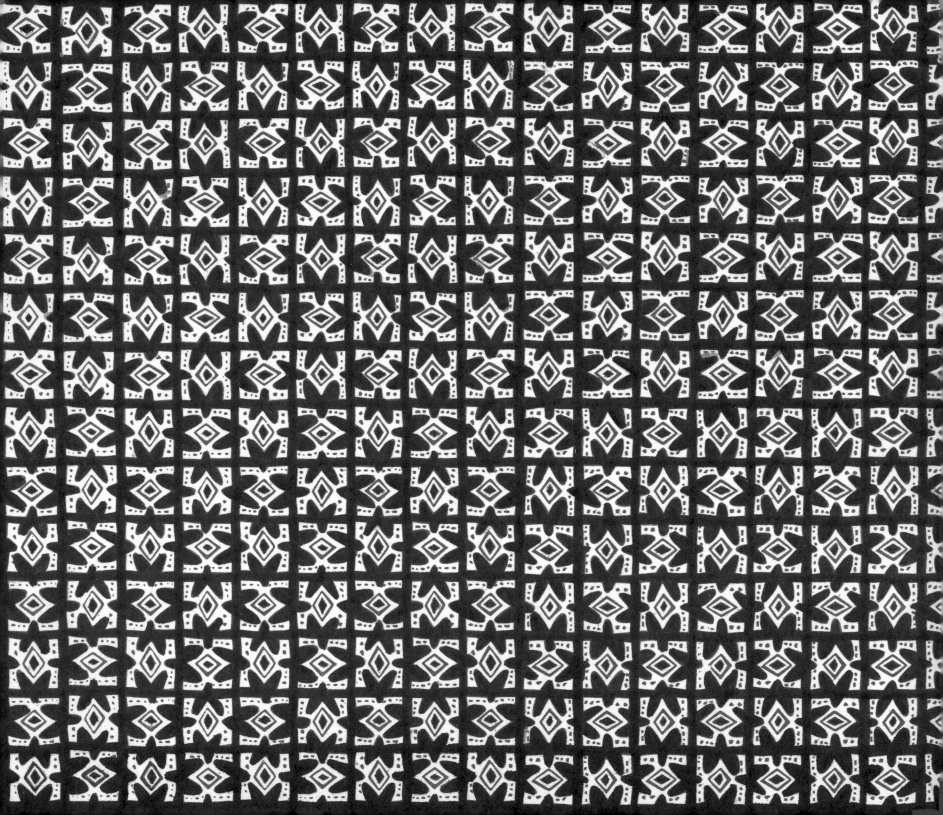